chains of love

and
other free verse poems

By Elliot M. Rubin

Copyright April 2020
Library of Congress

ISBN #978-1-7328493-6-5

Dedication
To Shane, Izzy, Jon, Carter,
Alex, Melanie, Mollie, and Madison

In Memory of
Herman S. Rubin
Who wrote poetry all his life.

Preface

A book of poetry can cover a lot of subjects.
Truth hurts sometimes but can also be healing.
I hope you enjoy the poems.

Table of Contents

chains of love

wanting to leave is hard-
he lost his lust for her
yet she remains,
her mind chained to him

the emotional links
are wrapped around
her heart, hard as steel,
it seems unbreakable

until he moves on,
destroys her soul-
she will stay, forever
moaning his betrayal

unsure of the future
she fights the urge-
mentally staying with him
until she is awakened

a new, powerful love
from heaven
traipsed into her life
she did not expect

cutting the chains
freeing her to leave,
to begin anew
without him

only a beer

the dive bar is dark,
from the rear the
grunge band
plays hard rock
damaging eardrums

a young woman
approaches,
small talk at first
then asks for a drink,
expecting a treat
due to her wide smile

the strobes light up
colorful small butterflies
tattooed on her arms,
birds on her neck,
a spread wing golden eagle
boldly sitting across
her opened shirt chest

i said no
when asked
if i want her
to be my bitch
cause i already
have a forever girl

i only wanted a beer
after work, not
an adventure-
sometimes it's
best to just
walk away

protein and carbs

in middle age
he walked out
leaving her with two
fifteen-year-old dogs;
plus divorce papers
on the nightstand
in the morning
when she woke up

months later,
she saw him online
with his teenage lover
hugging, kissing walking
hand in hand somewhere
on a beach with palm trees

depressed,
she went for her favorite
comfort food,
sat at
a small table,
opened a book, then
orders meatballs and spaghetti
with a glass of red wine

dating is hard;
trying to find
the same type man
as her husband,
except one who will love her

bad dates, terrible dates;
depressed
the waiter brings her gelato, gratis-

he knew she came in often
by herself, then read,
eat, linger awhile
reading a book of poetry
while sipping Bordeaux-
she looks up, decides to
leave her number
with a note for him

if you decide not to call,
next time i come in
act like it never happened;
i don't want to not come back
to eat the meatballs and spaghetti
i love so much

he did call,
is nothing
like her husband,
they start to date,
everything goes well

after a few months
they break up

she still goes back
for her delicious
protein and carbs,
with a book of poetry

action

i do not know
the height
i'll go,
or the depth
in life
i'd sow

i saw her
standing there,
fingers twirling
in her hair

imagination
laid her bare,
do i act, or
do i not

dare

endings

September wind blows
forests naked, all alone
she boards the noon train

***

leaves fall from the trees
after the summer season,
forlorn, she looks out

***

they exchanged gold rings
love was to be forever
tears fell when ended

***

pollen floats in air
love flies high; divorce ends it
lost souls fall to earth

***

sitting on the train
slowly a vial is opened,
the coach leaves forever

a swimming mind

walking in the surf
of creativity
a tidal wave
engulfs me,
pushing me forward

i can't stop
or swim out
it keeps my mind
focused,
possesses me,
forcing my hands
to entomb it
on paper
for others to enjoy,
to swim with me
for years to come
even after i'm gone

friendship

depressed
after his wife died,
he too is elderly,
alone,
missing her

shopping, pushing
a food cart
he passes
a five-year-old girl
with outreached arms,
asking for a hug

a friendship blooms
with weekly walks,
going to kindergarten
graduation,
both are in pictures

in the hospital
she still visits,
gives hugs
to her friend

the next day
with a smile
on his face
he joined
his wife

not done yet

i'm not ready
to back down-
there is still much
i want to do
though the years
are slipping away,
my life
is not yet finished

there is much love
i have to give-
an open heart
can receive as well;
new people
i have not yet met,
old friends
are still alive
in my memory

more thoughts
to write,
ideas not yet born,
i stare death in the face
not afraid,
challenging
my mind to
create
while i can

slipping away

he had it in his hands
but didn't realize how valuable
her love is until it slipped away,
walking out the door not looking back

it was a toxic relationship, shouting
at her, throwing things, verbally abusive,
insults also to his mother-
finally, he hit the limit, too much, too long

self-worth opened her eyes after a year
of therapy and group meetings-
the future is unknown,
nerve-racking but quiet,
peaceful,
allowing her to fly

graffiti on the wall - 2020

English Ph.D.'s
stood in silence,
motionless
their eyes reading
bubble letters

words put together
searing into their souls

linguists called in
are astounded
at the simple
complexity
of the word string

reporters present,
video too,
capturing a message
someone spray-painted
on a brick wall

**remember, remember
to vote in November**

virus

the dark
outshines
the light

people desperate
afraid with fright

running to hide

                iso-late

till a future
unknown date

the marriage highway

starting on mile one
the road ahead
looks smooth,
an easy ride
with no stops
planned
or expected

the curves
are gentle
sloping slightly
we handle them,
continue on our
journey
pedal to the floor

unseen potholes
make my grip
loosen causing us to
careen,
almost crashing-
an early end
to the trip

the journey continues-
our destination
insight;
old age
together,
holding hands
as we celebrate
a trip of over
fifty years
together

thinking in virus isolation

all you need to do
is grow old with me,
enjoy the mornings
together,
the sunsets
in each other's arms,
then face the end,
whatever it may be
in peace and tranquility

to my daughters

don't be
the woman
he wants-
be the woman
you want,
then
if he wants
you,
he will want
you

maturity

mumble words from his mouth
bumble the way he took out the ring
jumble a diamond in his hands
rumple is the way he's dressed

crumble to the floor in shock

she said yes to be his wife
rushing to marry for her life
standing by him alongside
being his new blushing bride

years later never had a say
till school changed her one fateful day
from then on it is her way
no longer to be his bae

my closed door

the door to my prison
is unlocked
yet i dare not open it

the danger on the other side
is both known and unknown-
it is unseen, deadly, sickening

at times, the four walls close in
with the only voice, i hear,
is from the king

he sits in a golden tower
with sycophants praising
him while i sit in depression

someday in the future, i hope
to open the door to freedom
the threat vanquished

and he is dethroned

a memory of a different door

sitting in a bistro
i order the fresh
Long Island oysters
cooked in a butter sauce

the handful of mollusks
have their shells shut,
tightly protecting them
from the elements

as the steam rises
the shells slowly
open their doors
exposing the interior

once pried open, giving up
the protected prize,
all is lost to the elements
with my fork and tongue

affair

variety
is the spice
of life

in viral times
keep the spices
in the closet

until a future
dish comes along
with the virus
long gone

prom night

the blue organza gown
slips off her body
slides to the floor
resting at her ankles
while he fumbles
behind her,
trying to
undo two small clips
on a strapless brassiere
after the prom is over

the hotel room curtains
are pulled closed
after he yanks the duvet
to the foot of the bed,
allowing her to climb
onto the crisp,
white linen sheets
to await her date

anticipating a drunken
night of lust,
teenagers
careen to adulthood

in the months ahead
they awake
to parenthood

gonna sing country

walking down the long dirt road
between cornfields on both sides;
she is intent on leaving him behind
to make it on her own in the city

a guitar strapped across her back
with songs she wrote secure
in her memory, the road to town
ends at the bus station ticket agent

arriving in the early evening she walks
out of the station and starts to sing
on the sidewalk as passerby's drop
money in her hat lying on the concrete

after a while she scoops up the hat
then stuffs cash in her jean jacket.
entering a cafe she orders a burger
and starts to count her earnings

amongst the money is a card from a
talent agent. scrawled on the card he
wrote to call him. excited, intending
to call when she found a motel to stay

walking down dark uunlit streets
her mind thinks about what to say.
she did not see a car coming toward her.
It misses as she steps back, but trips

a truck coming the other way
couldn't stop

today

today i put on my
virtual reality headpiece,
using it
to search
all over the house

upstairs, downstairs
in the basement;
everything is so realistic
i felt i could
almost touch everything;
except you are
still missing
from my life

tough decision

friends say i am weak
cause i fell in love
with you-
there are things
i cannot explain,
although you
have tried,
failed, and
did not give up
attempting
to stop me

i know you are with
another
yet i cannot
help myself

was it a fling
to you,
a momentary lapse
in a relationship,
did you mean it
all those times
when you said
you wanted me
to be yours forever

i know you are
attracted to us both,
but you need to choose;
her or me

i can't go on like this
cause i love you

instagram lamentation

love from afar,
on line
is difficult;
especially
when we never met

i don't know
where she lives;
poems, words, and pictures
are how we communicate
.

real names
are hidden
behind aliases

not being able
to extend my hand
to caress her,
kiss her,
physical bodies merging
leaves me frustrated-
the only way
she can feel me
is through her heart,
as mine also yearns
for her love in return

alas, it will never be;
as rosaline
is to romeo,
i am with my juliet

the rebbe

he sat there watching,
listening, as hundreds
of followers chanted in
unison a Hasidic melody

his long beard grey with
age, eyes furrowed from
years of reading and prayers,
he spoke words of wisdom

his goal is to send out missionaries
to the four corners of the world;
bringing Jews back to his version
of Judaism, with love and understanding

he said the messiah is coming soon;
some thought he was the one who
came to save the world, though he
never claimed the title nor denied it

memories of a sleepover

as a young boy my grandmother
would pick me up from kindergarten
and bring me to her apartment
over my dad's store for lunch

she would smoke unfiltered Camel
cigarettes, drink black Maxwell House
coffee, listen to As The World Turns
on the radio, while she told me stories

one night i slept over in the front bedroom,
with shades down the lights from traffic
flashed across them, hearing the trolley car
wheels grind on the embedded steel tracks

my grandfather slept in the next bed while
grandma's room is in the rear. i never spoke
to him until he moved in with us years later,
after she died. i was in high school by then

nothing important happened that night;
except a memory was created which
flashes back occasionally when i'm alone,
reminding me of my beloved grandmother,
and my eyes tear up

a walk in isolation

my knee felt good this morning,
arthritis is sleeping
i'm pain-free-
looking out
i see the fine misty rain
has stopped
leaving a sheen of gloss
on black asphalt streets-
putting on sneakers
i start the first
of my three daily walks.
as the road twists and turns
i am alone
this early morning;
i start to think of
my bar mitzvah 61 years ago-
the Hazon opens the curtain
of the Aron Chodesh
lifting a Torah out, placing
it on the table.-
he unrolls to the day's portion
then calls up to the bemah
two readers-
when it's my turn.
i start to recite three required prayers
when i look up
at the filled sanctuary,
spotting my grandfather
sitting with my parents-
tears are streaming down his face
as i carry on the tradition
of the family he left behind
years ago in Europe;
remembering those slaughtered

in the woods by Nazis-
a car wakes me
from my thoughts
as i step to the side
of the road
letting both the vehicle
and my thoughts pass along

bravery

a soldier running
directly
into withering gunfire
to defend his country
is not fearless
but brave-
firemen running
into the World Trade Center
as it collapses
trying to save people
are not fearless
but brave-
wives shopping
for food
to feed families
while a pandemic rages
are not fearless
but brave-
a uniform
is not the only thing
required for bravery,
you need
a heart big enough
to care for others
before yourself

maturity

hold me, i'm slipping away
i can't stay here another day
where did your love for me go
things changed i can sense it

you seem distant, uninterested
in being with me any longer.
after all these years together
i am the same, you changed

you grew, confident, self-assured
i feel i cannot keep up; i fell behind.
maybe someday you'll look back
thinking of what we had, i doubt it

you spread your wings
flying high and fast-
i'll miss you forever,
forever i will miss you

a writing poet

sitting at her desk
the poet wrote
of feelings,
desires, and
lost loves
who walked away
to be with others

although she is cute
the bad boys
she's attracted to
eventually leave
for the bimbos
with figure-eight bodies
and zero brains

her tats tell a life story
with the men's faces
on her legs, arms, back,
plus one near her honeypot

used, abused, beat down
she always picks herself up,
vowing never to date the same
type guy again-
after a few nights alone
she looks for a short term
companion;
afterward, they seem
to hang around
repeating the cycle
over again

her words on paper
fly off the page
a diary of sorts
helps her cope-
one-day things changed-
a magazine
hired her to write;
her male coworkers
look like the same
type of man,
except they are literate,
kind, treat her well.
even the one
she now dates
who loves exploring
her tats
while gently
kissing and caressing
her body,
except he does it
with respect

easter haiku

she dates lots of men
but for lent decided to
give up abstinence

feelings in isolation

my world lives
on in my mind-
the carefree days
of youth long gone
imprisoned
in my home unless
i gamble
with illness and death

talking to friends
is over electronics
not face to face
preventing me
from meeting new people
or having new experiences
in the world
outside my home

the question is,
who is to blame?
a national viral epidemic
killing thousands
needs a federal response,
not a localized one
state by state

i know whom to blame for incompetence,
i know who is endangering my family,
i know who not to vote for in november,
i know, do you?

up in smoke

smoke from the cigarette
dangling from his lips
spirals up
twisting in the breeze
as he leans against
a light pole
waiting
for his date to arrive

in the distance
he hears
the rumble
of a Harley
as it turns the corner
heading toward him,
stopping
in front of the pole
the engine stops
as she lowers the kickstand
then hops off the bike

she's dressed in black leather
from boots
to her skin-tight tee-shirt;
he offers his cigarette
to drag on
after she takes off her helmet
allowing long, straight, black hair
to fall down her back
resting on her shoulder

they walk in the bar
two doors down
sitting in a darkened corner booth

he reaches across the table,
places his hand over hers
then tells her
to drive him back
to his place
because he bought
new black leather
wrist and ankle cuffs
for her to wear
in his bedroom

pulling her hand back
she tells him
that she is no longer
his sex bitch
who sees him
whenever he wants

she found someone else
who wants a real relationship

then tells him
to walk home
as she stands,
walking out the door

why?

children are crying
mom lost her job
her company closed
food is running out

a single mother
what does she do
buy food or pay
the landlord's rent?

the decision is delayed-
she has a fever and cough,
tests positive sent to ER
leaving her kids home, alone

child protective services
places them in foster care
while she is in quarantine
for sixty days fighting for life

flat on a bed in a hallway
tubes, wires going in and out-
hundreds of people on the floor
she asks god a question, "why?"

amongst dozens of strangers
she dies alone, never getting an answer;
reporters ask her question to POTUS
only to be mocked and insulted

incompetence has no answers

high stakes

he is the ultimate
gambler, risking
his backer's money
in a high stakes
game of chance

remorseless
if he loses the stakes
of his backers,
he bets on hunches
instead of tried and true
gambling systems
and procedures
which worked in the past

when all the chips are in
and there is nothing left
to gamble with, the virus
will have won, and we die

a new world

everywhere you look
the men and women
are youthful,
zestful
heads full of hair
teeth gleaming white
babies in carriages
walking with parents

something is missing

there are no elderly
anywhere,
none to be seen-
years ago there were
grandparents,
seniors,
retired folks
everywhere,
unfortunately
none survived

the trump virus killed them all

mixed

it is a mixed marriage-
her full,
sensual
red lips,
pursed and ready,
correlates with her
curvy olive-toned
latina body
wearing a tight
body-hugging dress

contrasting with
his pencil
thin, white
anglo-saxon
protestant
european
pink lips,
with a tall
sleek shape,
clothes
drape loosely
on his torso

when hearts merge
nothing else matters

country girl

she turned down
his proposal
cause her plans
were not marriage,
babies,
or tied down
with a loser

finally
getting off the farm
she went to the city,
alone,
with no skills
except for her voice,
trying to sing
for a living

living at the Y
she managed to earn cash
as a waitress;
her perky accent
and easy smile
helped earn big tips

it wasn't a smooth step
up the ladder
to success,
she never made it big-
one day she met
the tall, dark stranger
of fabled stories,
married him
babies followed

years later
in self-meditation
she longed
for open fields,
the simple life
of backcountry
she left
many years before,
now realizing
the quiet life
back home
was a good life
she already
had been living

he said

i never saw the memo
in November
i never saw the memo
i December
i never saw the memo
in January
i finally saw the memo
in March

after thousands of us died

midnight romance

the empty bungalow
at the top of the hill
was the perfect place
to bring her at midnight

teenagers are in love
with the concept of love,
but hormones always
overrules common sense

it's been almost sixty years
since we dated, but she still
meets me at midnight now
then, until i wake up at dawn

remember in november

a large hospital
has a full morgue,
a filled forty foot
refrigerated trailer;
they don't know
where to store the
dead people

to be clear, i said
dead people-
not dead bodies
not dead patients
but dead people,
lives that had value

your grandparents
your mother or father
your husband or wife
your child or grandchild

not once did the president
offer any heartfelt empathy-
his only concern is the economy,
he values money over our lives

and his re-election
in november,
to stay out of jail

temptation

i see her body,
sensuous,
teasing,
long wavy hair
draped
over her breasts
hiding them,
yet calling
for her body
to be ravished
if we ever meet

thin legs
crossed
at her ankles
hiding
her treasure;
teasing,
driving
men crazy
with lust

toying with
male emotions
as lilith does
to her victims
before she
devours
their souls;
digesting them
in eternal flames
of frustration
and regret

2020 reality

the tax cut and jobs act is
a drastic tax cut for the one percent
with a pittance cut for working-class,
as billion-dollar firms now pay nothing

if the cuts for each class is reversed
more mothers would have food for kids,
families could be paying rent until back
to work, and billionaires pay something

but Trumpists work for the wealthy,
trying to destroy healthcare for plain
folks, while companies donate big bucks
to right-wing political action committees

wake up, wake up, stop drinking
the kool-aid before they kill us all,
as they retreat to their yachts, estates,
or hard to reach apartments in the sky